Holding the Pencil

Encourage your child to hold the pencil properly. The child should hold the pencil gently in between the thumb and the forefinger, about 1 or 2 cm above the tip.

The pencil should rest on the middle finger for proper support. This gentle grip allows the child to move the pencil easily for smooth writing movements.

Left hand

This book will help you to observe which hand the child favors. If your child is left-handed, tilt the page at a clockwise angle so that the top left corner is slightly higher than the right. Place the paper slightly to the left of the child's body to prevent smudging of letters.

Right hand

Keep your hand relaxed.

Bend your fingers, not your arm.

Don't press the pen too hard.

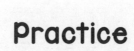

Practice

The handwriting of your child will improve if you encourage them to practice their motor skills constantly. You can encourage them to write on the sand, color the letters or cut letters with safety scissors.

Standing Lines

Trace the dotted lines from top to bottom.

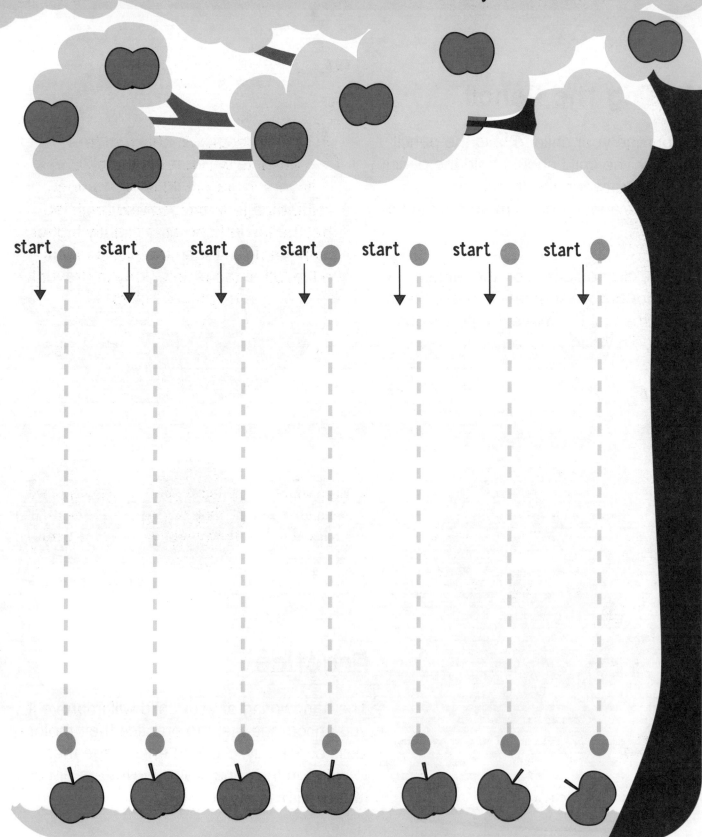

Sleeping Lines

Trace the dotted lines from left to right.

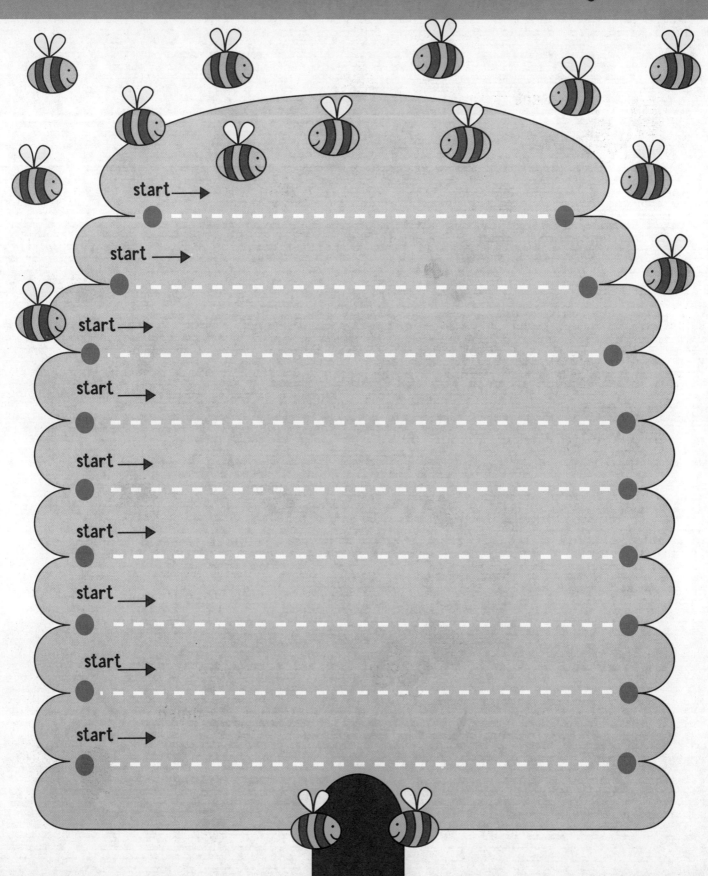

start →

start →

start →

start →

start →

start →

start →

start →

start →

Dog Path

Help the dog reach his home by drawing a line within the path given below.

start →

finish

Zig-Zag Lines

Trace the dotted lines on the crocodile's back.

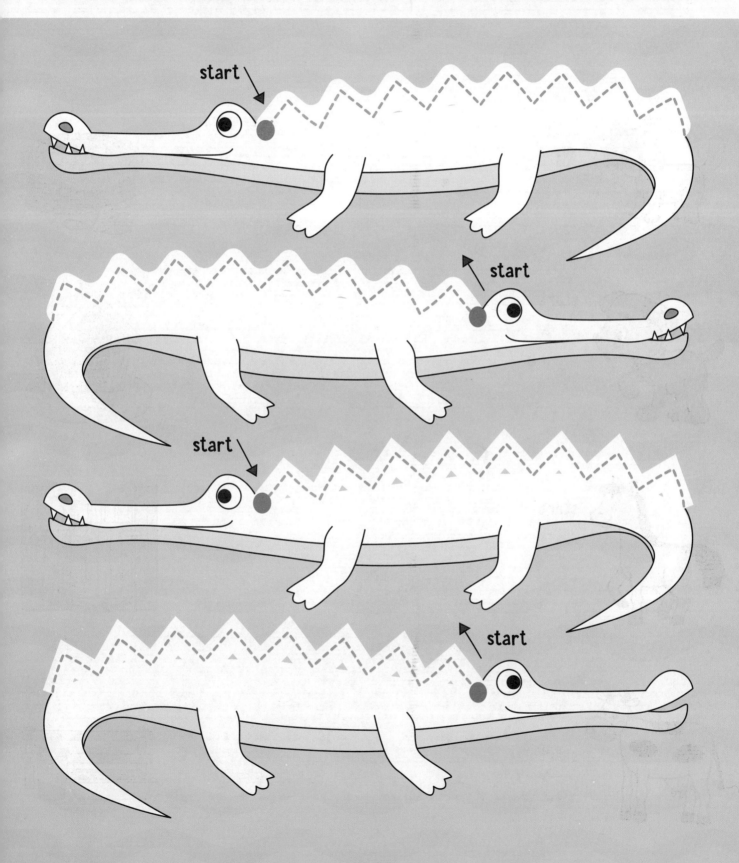

Way to Home

Trace the lines from the animals to their homes.

start →

start

start

start →

Wavy Lines

Trace the wavy lines to match the pictures.

Autumn Foliage

Trace the path of the falling leaves and acorns.

start

start

Curved Lines

Trace the dotted lines to complete the picture.

Spiral Patterns

Trace the spiral lines and complete the snails.

Blooming Tulips

Trace the spiral lines and complete the tulips.

Basic Shapes

Trace the dotted lines and complete the patterns.

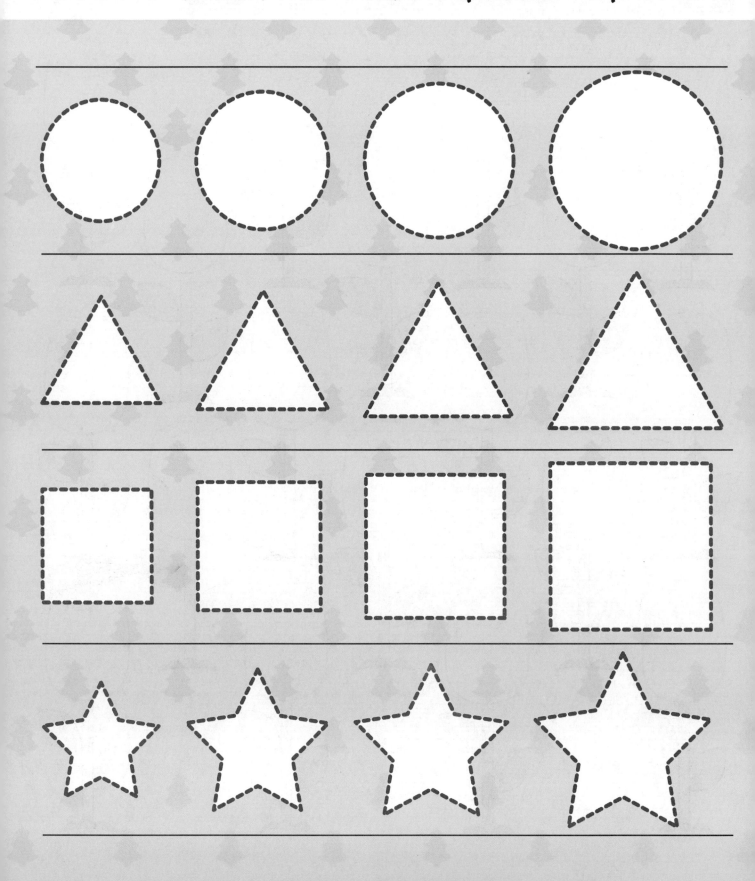

A Colorful Train

Trace the dotted lines and complete the train.

Lines and Vehicles

Trace the lines and match the vehicles.

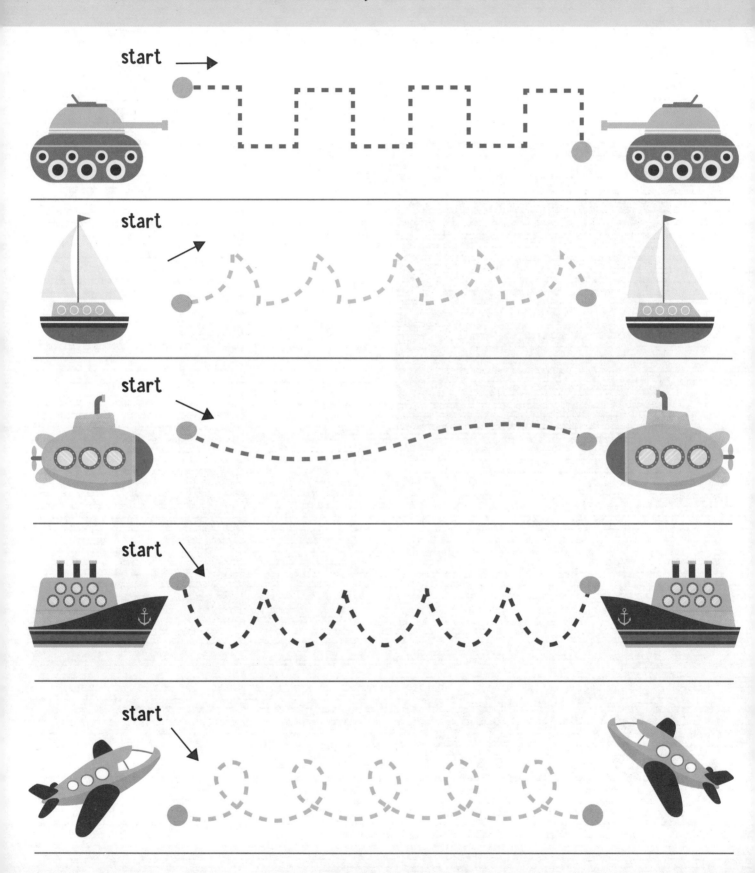

Busy Bees

Trace the lines and help the bees reach the flowers.

BaLLoon Strings

Trace the balloon strings and complete the picture.

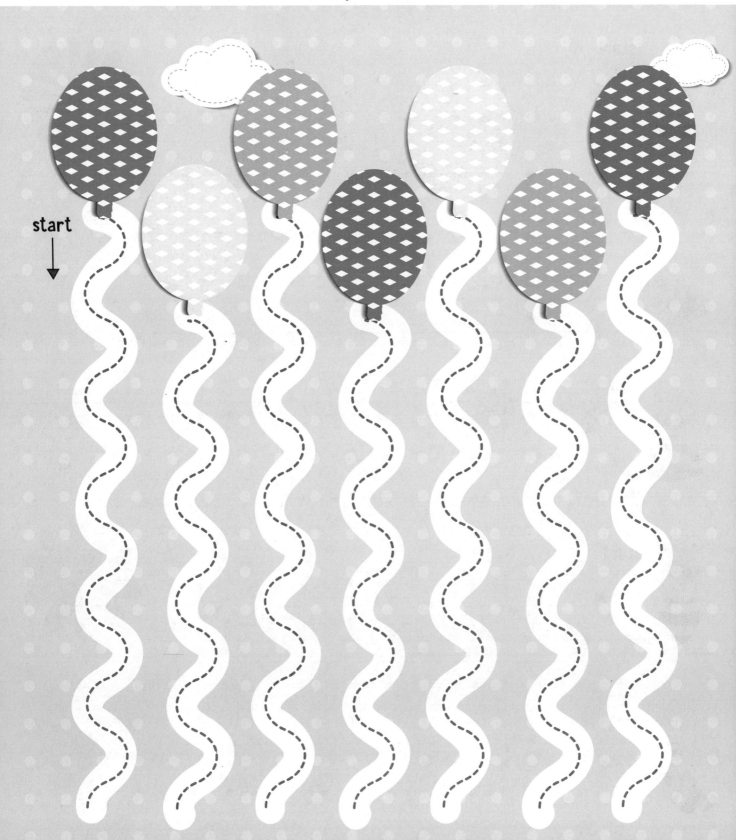

start